MICHAEL DAHL PRESENTS

THE BRAVE LITTLE TAILOR

A GRIMM AND GROSS RETELLING

BY J. E. BRIGHT

ILLUSTRATED BY TIMOTHY BANKS

STONE ARCH BOOKS
a capstone imprint

Michael Dahl Presents is published by Stone Arch Books,
A Capstone Imprint
1710 Roe Crest Drive
North Mankato, Minnesota 56003
www.mycapstone.com

Library of Congress Cataloging-in-Publication Data
Names: Bright, J. E., author. | Banks, Timothy, illustrator.
Title: The brave little tailor : a Grimm and gross retelling / by J. E. Bright
   ; illustrated by Timothy Banks.
Description: North Mankato, Minnesota : Stone Arch Books, [2018] | Series:
   Michael Dahl presents. Grimm and gross | Summary: In this humorous
   adaptation of the Grimm fairy tale, Abe Spoke is the young tailor who sews
   the words "seven in one stroke" on his belt, but neglects to tell the
   people he meets that it was seven flies, not seven giants—his cleverness
   (and chutzpah) win him the hand of the princess, but unfortunately he has
   a bad habit of muttering about cloth and tailoring in his sleep.
Identifiers: LCCN 2018013829 (print) | LCCN 2018017896 (ebook) | ISBN
   9781496573230 (eBook PDF) | ISBN 9781496573155 (hardcover) | ISBN
   9781496573193 (pbk.)
Subjects: LCSH: Fairy tales—Adaptations. | Tailors—Juvenile fiction. |
   Giants—Juvenile fiction. | Truthfulness and falsehood—Juvenile fiction.
   | Humorous stories. | CYAC: Fairy tales. | Tailors—Fiction. |
   Giants—Fiction. | Honesty—Fiction. | Humorous stories. | LCGFT: Humorous
   fiction. | Fairy tales.
Classification: LCC PZ8.B67616 (ebook) | LCC PZ8.B67616 Br 2018 (print) |
   DDC
   [Fic]—dc23
LC record available at https://lccn.loc.gov/2018013829

Editor: Eliza Leahy
Designer: Bob Lentz
Production Specialist: Tori Abraham

Printed in Canada.
PA020

MICHAEL
DAHL
PRESENTS

Michael Dahl has written about werewolves, magicians, and superheroes. He loves funny books, scary books, and mysterious books. Every Michael Dahl Presents book is chosen by Michael himself and written by an author he loves. The books are about favorite subjects like monster aliens, haunted houses, farting pigs, or magical powers that go haywire. **Read on!**

TABLE OF CONTENTS

WARNING!

Did you know that flies have to vomit on their food before eating it, dissolving it into runny liquid they can suck up through their tongues? I do now, after reading this retelling of the Grimm folktale. Yeech! The flies are only the beginning. They land on young Abe's slurpy jam sandwich, and it's all downhill from there. And please—don't ask me what giants eat. You'll find out for yourself in chapter two.

 **=** # GRIM

The Grimm brothers were known for writing some *GRIM* tales. Look for the thumbs-down and you'll know the story is about to get grim.

 **=** # GROSS

Luckily there's also a lot of *GROSS* stuff in this story. Look for the thumbs-up to see when it's about to get gross.

---

1. These are footnotes. Get it? Dr. Grossius Grimbus, researcher of all things grim and gross, shares his highly scientific observations.

CHAPTER ONE
SQUISH!

GURRRGGGLE!

A young little tailor named Abraham Spoke heard his stomach rumbling. "I will finish this belt before lunchtime," he promised himself.

Abe was an apprentice until a few weeks ago. His master, Giuseppe Couturier, accidentally ate a deadly mushroom and rotted away. Giuseppe had been a cruel man. He made old-fashioned clothes. Nobody missed him.

Now the small tailor shop belonged to Abe. Whistling, Abe sewed a strip of leather onto a wide, green velvet belt. He had a fancy jacket that matched. Sunlight streamed inside the open window. It helped him clearly see his fine stitches.

"Good jams! Cheap!" a woman called from the street. Abe licked his lips and leaned out the window. The jam seller wore a purple hooded cloak. She held a woven basket.

"I am hungry for jam, good woman!" called Abe.

The woman came over to the window. She was trailed by a cloud of buzzing flies. Abe raised an eyebrow when he saw the woman's face. Should he tell her about the big spider on her cheek? Soon he was glad he hadn't. It was a hairy wart!

Abe took his time opening the jars and

sniffing. Most of them were nasty. He sniffed
crab apple, stinging nettle, frog's eye,
bog-mallow, pea, eel, and toe. The plum jam
was the only one that didn't smell gross. He
bought a small jar. The woman's hand crawled
with flies as she took his money.

Abe's stomach growled again. He spread
plum jam on a slice of bread. Then he glanced
at his half-sewn belt. "I should finish before
I eat," Abe decided. He placed the bread on
the table. His fingers sewed faster as the sweet
smell of the jam teased his nose.

But the flies hadn't left. Dozens swarmed inside.

BUZZ!

"Hey!" Abe cried. "Who invited you?" He tried to shoo the bugs away.

The flies landed on the bread and tasted the plum jam with their feet. They vomited on his lunch. This turned the jam into runny liquid. The flies sucked it up with their tongues.[1]

"Ew, that's vile!" yelled Abe. He grabbed the belt and raised it high. "Disgusting creatures!"

1. According to my observations, this revolting method is how flies eat. Their repulsive puke breaks down food. Then they vacuum it up with their horrible mouthparts.—Dr. Grossius Grimbus

He slapped the belt down on the flies.

SPLAT!

Quite a few flies lay crumpled and smashed like raisins. Their skinny legs twitched.

Abe counted the dead. He'd killed seven. With a single smack!

He puffed up his chest. He was impressed with his own bravery and skill. "This is most bragworthy," he told himself. "I should tell the whole town!"

Suddenly Abe had an idea. He brushed flecks of fly guts and wing bits off the belt.

He cut four words out of yellow silk. Then he sewed the letters onto the belt in his fanciest stitching.

SEVEN WITH ONE SMACK

Abe adjusted the velvet jacket. He strapped the belt around his waist. Now everyone he met would read about his courage. He gobbled the rest of his lunch.

"Forget this tiny town," Abe said. "It's not big enough for my huge heroism." The little tailor's heart thumped with pride. Or possibly he had an upset stomach. "I shall bring news of my bravery to the whole wide world!"

CHAPTER TWO
GIANT TRICKS

Abe looked around his shop for rations. He found a round cheese in the cupboard and put it in his jacket pocket.

Abe whistled as he stepped outside. He left the door unlocked because he would never return. Down the path, he saw a fluttering sparrow stuck in a shrub.

He pulled the bird free. *A bird in the hand is worth two in the bush,* he thought. He put the bird in his pocket too.

With a joyful spring in his step, Abe hurried out of town.

SPROING!

He strolled along a dirt road that climbed a forested mountain. After hours of hiking, Abe neared the peak. A disgusting stench hit his nose. Flies buzzed around. Abe tried to identify the odor. A rotting whale? A bear with B.O. from ten years of hibernation? A freshly dug-up graveyard? None of those seemed bad enough.

Abe followed the flies around a twisted pine tree. On the other side was a hairy giant staring at the valley below. The huge brute's stink floated around him in a brown haze.

This giant is so strong and smelly. He'd make a great bodyguard on my adventures! Abe thought. The little tailor bravely strode over. "Good day, friend!" he shouted. "What's your name? I am Abraham, but you can call me Abe."

The giant peered down. "I am called Butte," he thundered. "What you want?"

Abe smiled. "I'm headed into the wide world to seek my fortune. Care to join me?"

The giant chuckled, which made the mountain tremble. "With you, pipsqueak?"

"Me, indeed!" Abe answered. He showed Butte his belt.

The giant squinted. "'Seven with one smack,'" he read. "Huh. That an impressive number of victims. But if you so powerful,

do this!" Butte grabbed a rock the size of Abe's head and squeezed it. Watery mud trickled out.

"Child's play!" replied the tailor. He pulled the cheese from his pocket. Then he squeezed it in his fist. Juice squirted out, and flies swarmed.

Butte tried not to act impressed. He picked up another stone and hurled it into the sky. It traveled so far that it fell on the next mountain.

"Well thrown," said Abe. "But mine will never return." He slid the sparrow out of his pocket. It squirted a streak of white waste onto Abe's hand. The tailor hurled the bird.

WHOOOOSHHHHH!

The sparrow flew away and didn't come back.

"Huh," said Butte. "You brave enough to spend night among giants?"

"I accept your invitation," said Abe. He followed the giant into the woods.

 Here's where it gets a little GROSS. . . .

Butte led Abe to a deep cavern. Inside there were six giants. They sat around a crackling fire. Each chomped messily on a roasted cow or sheep.

Butte introduced them. "This Belche, wife. Brother, Germey. Uncle Durt. Aunt Todestule. Other Aunt Rocky. And darling mother-in-law, Urmpitt."

CHOMP! CHOMP! CHOMP!

Grease and food bits spewed from the giants' mouths. Urmpitt grunted. She tossed a cow skull into the fire. Flies feasted on meat scraps. The giants' faces looked monstrous in the firelight. The beasts were covered with moss and filth. They wore soiled, stinking rags.

Abe smiled to show he wasn't afraid.

"You sleep now," said Butte. He pushed Abe to a big bed in the back of the cave.

Abe crawled onto the gigantic, leaf-stuffed mattress. He gathered the sticky fur covers into a bunch so it looked like he was sleeping in the center of the bed. Then he found a ledge of stone sticking out from the cave wall. He curled up beneath it.

 This is where it gets a bit GRIM!

Around midnight, Butte tiptoed over to Abe. The dying fire lit up the giant's shape. Butte raised a huge wooden club. Then he smashed the middle of the bed.

CRAAAASH!

"We eat his bones for breakfast," said Butte.

Abe fell sleep safe in his corner. The giants wouldn't bother him until first light.

The tailor woke early. He waited by the smoldering fire pit.

Aunt Rocky was the first to wake.

"Good morning," said Abe.

Aunt Rocky gawped. Then she let out a shriek.

AIIIEEEEEEEEHHHH!

"Ghost!" she hollered. "He kill us all! Seven with one smack!"

The other giants scrambled from their beds. They ran screaming into the forest.

Abe felt full of confidence. He continued his journey beyond the mountain.

CHAPTER THREE
THE KING'S CHALLENGE

Abe walked through farmland, past tiny towns, and along forest roads. Eventually he reached a stinky city called Kotzendorf. The streets oozed with filth. Flies swarmed. *This place needs a sewer system,* he thought. However, everyone Abe met was impressed with his Seven with One Smack triumph.

That night, Abe climbed a grassy hill on the edge of the city. The air was clearer atop

the hill. Abe had a great view of the city. He spotted a chunky castle with three towers poking up over a tall wall.

Abe followed cobblestone roads to the palace courtyard. He strode inside, past the snoozing guard.

Zzzzzzzzz!

Abe found a grassy spot outside the palace stables. Even horse manure smelled pleasant after the giants' cave. He lay down and had a good night's sleep.

When the tailor opened his eyes again, he was surrounded by city folk staring at him. "Good morning," Abe greeted them.

A well-dressed man nodded. "I am Ambassador Dongle," he said. His teeth were as yellow as a daffodil. "Our King Mumpitz welcomes you to Kotzendorf. Will you join our city's army?"

"Um . . . er . . . yes. That's why I'm here," stammered Abe. "I am ready to enter the king's service."

The citizens cheered.

"This is Mink," Ambassador Dongle

said. "He is a squire to the king. He will get you settled." He pushed forward a teenager with a pageboy haircut.

"Sir, please follow me to your new home," said Mink. He led Abe to a cottage in the soldiers' quarters. The inside smelled moldy, but it would do. Mink showed Abe the overgrown backyard, surrounded by a fence. They overheard soldiers talking next door.

"You were suspended, Grench?" asked one soldier.

"Aye," Grench grumbled. "For sleeping at the gate."

"You let that scary little warrior in," the other solider scolded. "He will strike us down. Seven with one smack!"

"What shall we do, Warren?" asked Grench. "I can't speak to King Mumpitz. He's mad at me for calling him 'Mommy' in my sleep."

"I'll talk to the king," said Warren.

Mink whispered to Abe, "I'll take you to face these cowardly soldiers in the king's court."

That afternoon, Mink led Abe into the throne room. Warren was already there, whining.

The throne room was made of dirty stone. It felt dank and dark. The walls were covered with hunting trophies. Flies circled the decaying animal heads.

Ambassador Dongle stood on the portly king's right side. On the king's left, a young princess sat in a chair. Abe thought she was

beautiful. She was so bored that she was
drooling.

Warren gulped when he saw Abe. But he squared his shoulders. "It is foolish to allow such a dangerous warrior in town. He can kill seven with one smack! Your military will rebel if he isn't sent away."

"I cannot lose my faithful soldiers," said King Mumpitz. He squirmed his large rump on the cushioned throne. The little tailor noticed that the king looked scared. His face was flushed dark red.

"He fears you are mighty enough to steal his throne," Mink whispered in Abe's ear.

"Sire, may I make a suggestion?" asked Abe. "Test my loyalty. Perhaps then you will feel comfortable welcoming me to Kotzendorf."

"Yes!" King Mumpitz said in relief. "There

are two giants in the forest who eat our sheep. They leave behind only the leftover hooves in the shepherds' fields." He shuddered and grew redder. "We asked them nicely to stop. The giants burned our wagons and spit on our soldiers. Conquer them to prove your worth. I will also give you half my kingdom and my daughter."

"Half your daughter?" asked Abe.

King Mumpitz fidgeted. "All of her," he said. "You may wed my daughter, Pricilla."

"Wait," said Princess Pricilla. She wiped her mouth. "What?"

"I accept your challenge," said Abe.

He knew the slippery king had made the offer because he thought it was an impossible feat. But the little tailor had dealt with giants before and won. He'd be a fool to miss this chance.

So Abe set out toward the dark forest. He was followed by Mink, a company of soldiers, and curious townsfolk. At the edge of the trees, the little tailor stopped. "Wait here," he said. "I will defeat the giants alone."

Abe entered the murky woods.

Heads-up . . . the next chapter gets a little **GRIM** *AND* **GROSS**.

CHAPTER FOUR
SOUR AND SWEET

Abe searched the woods. Soon he caught
a whiff of a sour smell. It stank of old milk,
vinegar, and filthy feet. Abe followed the
stench. He found two unwashed teenage giants
asleep under a massive oak tree. One had
red hair and shiny pimples all over his face.
The other had dirty yellow hair crawling with
green beetles.

Abe filled his pockets with stones. Then he
scrambled up the trunk of the oak. He settled
on a leafy limb above the giants.

The little tailor dropped a stone onto the redheaded giant's zitty forehead.

THUNK!

The ginger giant woke. He rubbed his brow. Zits popped in bursts of pus. He shoved the other giant. "Why you knock me?"

"You dreaming," grumbled the blond giant. He pulled a beetle out of his hair and ate it. "I not knock you."

The giants fell back asleep.

Abe dropped a rock onto the blond giant's head. The impact squished bugs and woke the giant.

He jostled the redhead. "Why you pelt me?"

"I not pelt you," whined the other.

"You pelt me!"

"You knock me!"

"No, now I knock you!" the yellow-haired giant yelled. He bonked the ginger giant with his fist. Pus squirted out.

The redhead sprang up. Furious, he grabbed the other giant. Then he slammed him against the oak trunk. Shiny beetles flung everywhere.

Abe held on as the tree shook.

Growling, the yellow-haired giant smashed the ginger one into a birch tree. The smaller tree splintered into smithereens.

The giants brawled. They scratched, walloped, bit, and punched. Their sour stink grew stronger as they sweated. Abe covered his nose and mouth to keep from gagging.

Finally the two giants smacked their heads together. The impact spewed snot out of their noses . . . and knocked them both out cold.

Abe climbed down the oak. He tied the giants up with vines. He avoided the pond of steaming snot. Then he strolled out of the woods to where the city folk waited.

"You're unhurt," said Mink, amazed.

"They didn't bend a hair of my head," said Abe.

The rejoicing citizens dragged the captured giants into the throne room. King Mumpitz looked shocked. His face turned redder than ever.

"Look, Daddy." Princess Pricilla pouted. She fanned the giants' sour stench away. "He lived."

"I have returned for my reward," Abe announced. "The giants are defeated."

"Not so fast," said King Mumpitz. "I still do not trust you. You must perform another heroic deed. Go again to the forest and capture the candy unicorn. This beast stabs holes in all our syrup and sugar barrels."

"I fear one candicorn less than two giants," replied Abe. "I will return with him."

With Mink's help, Abe got a barrel of sugar, a rope, and an ax. Then the little tailor led a group of merry citizens to the forest. Again he entered the woods alone. He rolled the sugar barrel between the trees.

Abe found a sunny field. He set the barrel upright. Then he hid behind a bush.

The candy unicorn rushed out of the forest. He was sugary white, with a fluffy pink mane. There was a sharp peppermint-striped horn on his forehead.

The candicorn thundered across the field.

A cloud of bees and flies followed him. He stabbed the barrel with his horn, sucking up all the sugar.[2] The candicorn looked around for something else to puncture and drain.

Abe got a whiff of the candicorn. The creature smelled sickly sweet, like scented candles, funeral flower bouquets, and rotten fruit. Abe remembered eating too much cotton candy at the fair when he was a little boy. He had barfed pink all night. Abe retched. He covered his mouth to stop the sound.

GAGGGGGGG!

The candicorn heard Abe. The muscular

2. Many scholars have noticed the horrific similarity of the way a candy unicorn—crassly called a candicorn by lesser zoologists—siphons sweets through its horn to the way a fly liquefies lunch and then sucks it up through its tubular tongue. I call this nonsense, as it implies a common horsefly ancestor. That is impossible and unscientific in the extreme.
—Dr. Grossius Grimbus

beast pawed the ground with his hoof. He hurtled toward the little tailor.

Abe stepped to the side. The candicorn rushed by in a mist of fruity perfume. "Too close for comfort," Abe said. "This time I'll be ready."

He hurried over to a fat-trunked maple. Abe stood with his back against the bark.

The candicorn whirled around in the field. He charged at Abe again. His hollow peppermint horn aimed to skewer the little tailor.

Abe waited until the last second. Right before the candicorn's horn hit him, he leaped to the side and rolled away.

The candicorn slammed his horn into the maple. The point jammed deep into the wood. The beast sucked maple syrup out of the tree.

GLUGG GLUGG GLUGGG!

Soon the tree was shriveled and empty. The candicorn tried to pull himself free. The trunk had shrunk and tightened. The candicorn was stuck! He pulled and twisted his horn. But he couldn't get loose.

Whistling merrily, the little tailor tied his rope around the candicorn's neck. He carefully hacked the wood around the horn with his ax. Eventually he freed the syrupy beast from the maple's trunk.

Abe led the captured candicorn out of the forest. The citizens hooted and hollered for their hero but kept their distance. They celebrated the whole way back to the castle and into the king's throne room.

King Mumpitz turned bright red again. He was obviously unhappy to see Abe.

"May I present this candicorn," said Abe. "It is my wedding gift for my new bride, Princess Pricilla."

The princess wiped her mouth. "Actually," she said, "that's quite nice."

King Mumpitz couldn't think of any way to wriggle out of his promise.

CHAPTER FIVE
THE DREAM

Abe and Pricilla's wedding in the castle courtyard was lovely. A huge crowd of Kotzendorf citizens attended. Everybody ignored the stink of sewage. Mink was Abe's best man. Princess Pricilla looked beautiful in her gown. She smiled at Abe when he kissed her, although her kiss was slobbery. Then the king threw a feast in the castle's dining hall. Abe avoided eating the green clams.

Ambassador Dongle rested a new prince's crown on the little tailor's head. Abe's joy spread throughout the city. They all danced late into the night.

Abe woke in the morning with the princess staring at him. Her chin dripped with saliva. "What is the matter, my wife?" he asked groggily.

"You spoke in your sleep, husband," said Princess Pricilla.

"Aha," said Abe. "Did I talk about fighting giants and candicorns, dear wife?"

"You were worried about trouser sizes," Pricilla explained. "You mumbled how cotton is better than wool for undergarments. You praised the strength of silk thread. Like you aren't a noble warrior at all . . . but some sort of . . . *ewww* . . . tailor."

Abe laughed. "Ha! Hahaha! Me, a tailor?"

"You designed my wedding dress," his wife pointed out.

"You never looked lovelier," said Abe. "I am just interested in fashion. A man is not responsible for his dreams, my dearest. Once I dreamed I had chicken wings. Nobody accused me of laying eggs!"

The princess argued with Abe no more. But he knew she still worried.

Mink visited Abe in the garden that afternoon. The little tailor was overseeing the construction of the candicorn's new habitat.

"I overheard something interesting," Mink whispered.

"It's a day for overhearing," replied Abe. "What have you learned?"

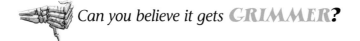 *Can you believe it gets* GRIMMER*?*

"The princess suspects you are not who you seem," said Mink. "She sobbed her fears to her father. It was very wet. The king said he'd send his guards to grab you tonight while you sleep. They plan to exile you across the ocean."

"Interesting indeed," said Abe. "Thank you, my friend."

After dark, the little tailor went to bed with Princess Pricilla. He pretended he knew nothing. He put the usual sponge beside his head to catch his wife's drool. Then he faked soft snoring so she would think he slept.

Pricilla slipped out of bed. She opened the chamber door to let in the king's guards.

"Silk is the strongest thread for throttling your enemies!" Abe cried out in his pretend sleep. "I killed seven with one smack. I defeated giants! I caught a candicorn! So what should I fear from anyone who dares enter my room? I shall squeeze their heads till they pop like pimples!"

The terrified guards ran like a hungry giant chased them.

Abe's fake dream also proved to his wife that he was a mighty warrior. The prince and princess had a long and pleasant marriage. They had many children.

King Mumpitz died from accidentally eating a deadly mushroom. The little tailor became King Abraham.

King Abraham always ignored the candicorn's flies that buzzed into his throne room. He ruled Kotzendorf wisely and so very bravely until the end of his days.

THE END

COMPARING THE TALES

J. E. Bright is a master of grossology, so when he starts his version of this Grimm tale, which begins with the tailor's lunch, Bright makes Abe's jam sandwich one of the grossest things I've ever read. And that's the reason I can never look at jam the way I used to. My brain keeps showing me those flies and their disgusting sucking tubes.

That's why, however, I thought Bright would be a perfect re-teller of this strange little story. He names one of the giants Belche, which is just the right touch. When the teen monsters fight in the forest, they bump heads together and "the impact spewed snot out of their noses!" At the tailor's wedding, the princess's kiss is surprisingly "slobbery." Yup, Bright knows gross.

He also knows his Grimm. In the original story, the princess does overhear her new husband talking in his sleep about sewing and other tailor-ish things. She suspects he is not the great warrior he claims to be. And, just like the original, Bright shows us Abe pretending to sleep the next night and mumbling about catching a unicorn and smiting his enemies. The princess is convinced she has married a valiant man. The same great Grimm ending. But I don't think the German brothers ever thought that their characters would end up with names like Dongle, Grench, and Urmpitt! Now that's gross.

—Michael

GLOSSARY

apprentice (uh-PRENT-ess) — a person who is learning a job by experience under a skilled worker

bragworthy (BRAG-wuhr-thee) — to be able to talk about how good you are at something

cowardly (COW-urd-lee) — lacking courage

dank (DANGK) — unpleasantly damp

heroism (HEIR-oh-wiz-uhm) — bravery

hibernation (hye-bur-NAY-shun) — a resting state used to survive poor conditions

impact (IM-pakt) — the action of one object coming into contact with another

monstrous (MON-struss) — large and frightening

pageboy (PAYJ-boy) — a haircut with straight, shoulder-length hair that's curled under at the ends

puncture (PUNK-cher) — to make a hole with a point

ration (RASH-uhn) — a set amount of something, like food, allotted to a person each day

smithereens (SMI-thuhr-eens) — small pieces

tailor (TAY-lur) — someone who makes or alters clothes

GROSSARY

DROOL (DROOL) — spit that drips from the mouth

FILTH (FILTH) — very dirty

GREASE (GREESS) — an oily substance found in animal fat and in hair and skin

MANURE (muh-NOO-ur) — animal waste

PIMPLE (PIM-puhl) — a small, raised spot on the skin that is sometimes painful and filled with pus

PUS (PUHSS) — a yellowish-white fluid found in sores and infections

RETCHED (RECHED) — made the sound or movement of vomiting

ROTTING (RAHT-ing) — something that is decaying

SALIVA (suh-LYE-vuh) — the clear liquid in your mouth that helps you swallow and begin to digest food

SOILED (SOYLED) — dirty or stained

STENCH (STENCH) — a strong, unpleasant smell

DISCUSS

1. Abe has to sleep in the giants' cavern. How would you feel if you had to sleep in such a gross place?

2. People think Abe is a brave warrior for getting "seven in one smack." Do you think the people would have been as impressed if they knew Abe's belt was talking about flies?

3. The candicorn is described as smelling both sweet and gross at the same time. Have you ever smelled something "sickly sweet?"

WRITE

1. Abe talks about tailor work in his sleep, which makes Pricilla worry. Write what you think would happen if Princess Pricilla found out Abe was a tailor.

2. Imagine Abe has to write to King Mumpitz explaining why he's worthy to marry Princess Pricilla. Pick one of Abe's adventures and describe it in a letter to the king.

3. Abe makes his battles seem greater than they were when telling them to other people. Write about a time you exaggerated like Abe did.

AUTHOR

J. E. BRIGHT is the writer of many novels, novelizations, and novelty books for children and young adults. He lives in the Clear Lake City suburb of Houston, Texas, with his cranky but cuddly female cat, Mabel, and his friendly dog, Henry. Find out more about J. E. Bright on his website.

ILLUSTRATOR

TIMOTHY BANKS is an award-winning artist and illustrator from Charleston, South Carolina. He's created character designs for Nike, Nickelodeon, and Cartoon Network, quirky covers for *Paste* magazine, and lots of children's books with titles like *There's a Norseman in My Classroom* and *The Frankenstein Journals*.

PHOBIA

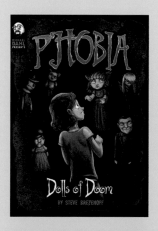

Dolls of Doom
BY STEVE BREZENOFF

The Creeping Clown
BY JESSICA GUNDERSON

The Haunted Dark
BY BRANDON TERRELL

The Monster in the Mirror
BY ANTHONY WACHOLTZ

only from capstone